The Night Before Christmas

CLEMENT CLARKE MOORE (1779–1863)
Author of "The Night Before Christmas"
Portrait painted late in life for the General Theological Seminary

The Night Before Christmas

(A Visit from St. Nicholas)

CLEMENT C. MOORE

Facsimile of the Original 1848 Edition

With a Life of Moore by
ARTHUR N. HOSKING

Dover Publications, Inc.
New York

Published in Canada by General Publishing Company, Ltd., 30 Lesmill Road, Don Mills, Toronto, Ontario.

Published in the United Kingdom by Constable and Company, Ltd.

This Dover edition, first published in 1971, is an unabridged and unaltered republication of the work originally published by Dodd, Mead & Company, New York, in 1934 with the title *The Night Before Christmas: The True Story of "A Visit from St. Nicholas"; With a Life of the Author Clement C. Moore Written by Arthur N. Hosking.* An appendix containing a reproduction of a manuscript of *The Night Before Christmas* in Clement C. Moore's own hand appears at the end of this edition.

International Standard Book Number (paper): 0-486-22797-9

Library of Congress Catalog Card Number: 79-165390

Manufactured in the United States of America
Dover Publications, Inc.
180 Varick Street
New York, N. Y. 10014

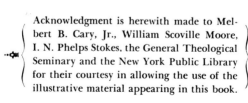
Acknowledgment is herewith made to Melbert B. Cary, Jr., William Scoville Moore, I. N. Phelps Stokes, the General Theological Seminary and the New York Public Library for their courtesy in allowing the use of the illustrative material appearing in this book.

FOREWORD

Mᴏʀᴇ than a century ago, the author of the "yellow and frail little sixteen-page pamphlet," here reproduced in facsimile, read his Christmas verses for the first time to his own children, before the fire-place in his New York home. Since that dim year, children, old and young, throughout the world, have turned, again and again, to the great good humor, the warmth and the kindly spirit of "A Visit from St. Nicholas" to catch once more the rich savor of life's most gracious day. No wonder that children, on Christmas Eve, sing carols over the last resting-place of Clement C. Moore!

Poems have been written which critics and scholars tell us are made of the authentic stuff of immortality. The little poem, reclaimed within the following pages, as it appeared long ago in the first, separate, quaint formality of "book publication," needs neither critic nor scholar to identify for us its immortality. We know it lives and is good, because it sings always in our hearts.

The succeeding sixteen pages are a facsimile of
"A Visit from St. Nicholas,"
owned by Melbert B. Cary, Jr.

SANTA CLAUS

SANTA CLAUS'S

VISIT.

A

VISIT FROM
ST. NICHOLAS.

BY

CLEMENT C. MOORE, LL.D.

With Original Cuts,

DESIGNED AND ENGRAVED BY BOYD.

New-York:

HENRY M. ONDERDONK,
10 John street.

1848.

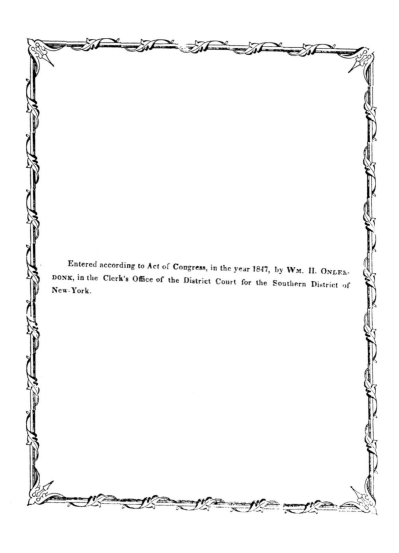

A

PRESENT

FOR

GOOD

LITTLE BOYS

AND

GIRLS.

VISIT FROM SANTA CLAUS.

'T WAS the night before Christmas,
    when all through the house
Not a creature was stirring, not
    even a mouse ;
The stockings were hung by the
    chimney with care,
In hopes that St. Nicholas soon
    would be there ;
The children were nestled all snug
    in their beds,
While visions of sugar-plums danced in their
    heads ;
And Mamma in her 'kerchief and I in my cap,
Had just settled our brains for a long winter's
    nap ;

When out on the lawn there arose such a clatter,

I sprang from the bed to see what was the
matter.

Away to the window I flew like a flash,

Tore open the shutters and threw up the sash.

The moon on the breast of the new-fallen snow,

Gave the lustre of mid-day to objects below,

When, what to my wondering eyes should appear,

But a miniature sleigh, and eight tiny rein-deer,

With a little old driver, so lively and quick,

I knew in a moment it must be St. Nick.

More rapid than eagles his coursers they came,

And he whistled, and shouted, and called them
by name;

" Now, *Dasher !* now, *Dancer !* now, *Prancer*
　　and *Vixen !*

On, *Comet !* on, *Cupid !* on, *Donder* and *Blit-
　　zen !*

To the top of the porch ! to the top of the
　　wall !

Now dash away ! dash away ! dash away
　　all !"

As dry leaves that before the wild hurricane
　　fly,

When they meet with an obstacle, mount to
　　the sky ;

So up to the house-top the coursers they flew,

With the sleigh full of Toys, and St. Nicholas
　　too.

And then in a twinkling, I heard on the roof,

The prancing and pawing of each little hoof—

As I drew in my head, and was turning around,

Down the chimney St. Nicholas came with a bound.

He was dressed all in fur, from his head to his foot,

And his clothes were all tarnished with ashes and soot ;

A bundle of Toys he had flung on his back,

And he looked like a pedlar just opening his pack.

His eyes — how they twinkled ! his dimples, how merry !

His cheeks were like roses, his nose like a cherry !

His droll little mouth was drawn up like a bow,

And the beard of his chin was as white as the snow ;

The stump of a pipe he held tight in his teeth,

And the smoke it encircled his head like a
wreath ;

He had a broad face and a little round belly,

That shook when he laughed, like a bowlfull
of jelly.

He was chubby and plump, a right jolly old elf,

And I laughed when I saw him, in spite of
myself,

A wink of his eye and a twist of his head,

Soon gave me to know I had nothing to dread ;

He spoke not a word, but went straight to his
work,

And fill'd all the stockings ; then turned with a
jerk,

And laying his finger aside of his nose,

And giving a nod, up the chimney he rose;

He sprang to his sleigh, to his team gave a whistle,

And away they all flew like the down of a thistle.

But I heard him exclaim, ere he drove out of sight,

"HAPPY CHRISTMAS TO ALL, AND TO ALL A GOOD NIGHT"

THE LIFE OF

CLEMENT CLARKE MOORE

BY

ARTHUR N. HOSKING

CHELSEA HOUSE

*The Homestead in which the poem was written and first read
in the year* 1822

Not long ago a stranger walked into the office of an acquaintance of mine and placed on his desk a yellow and frail little sixteen-page pamphlet and said: "Will you give me five dollars for this?" The acquaintance looked at the stranger and then at the pamphlet with what we may call commercial suspicion; but having a nose for rare things, my acquaintance, whose eye caught the simple title *Santa Claus* emblazoned on the cover, picked up the unusual booklet and examined it with the eye of the connoisseur, lingered on the naïve half-dozen woodcuts, and finally took out his wallet, handed the caller a ten dollar bill and said, "Why yes, I'll take it. Keep the change."

The seller, who was undoubtedly in need of funds, drew himself up, hesitated, but finally accepted the bill and disappeared as suddenly as he had come. He has never been seen since.

A short while after this transaction, my acquaintance placed the little book on my desk and with a whimsical smile asked:

"What do you think of it?"

This episode serves to introduce the story that follows.

THE perennial charm of the verses beginning with the strangely inspired line "'Twas the night before Christmas when all through the house" led me into a captivating realm of folk-lore quite unknown to me prior to the episode dealing with this one romance of books. Nowhere could I find a duplicate copy of this pamphlet, the title-page

[4]

of which read: "A Visit from St. Nicholas," by Clement C. Moore, LL.D.,—not in great public libraries, imposing historical societies, in the private holdings of book collectors, nor on the shelves of well-known rare-book dealers. No one to whom I showed the copy had ever seen its like before. Here was romance in connection with a poem which has been reprinted perhaps more often than any other poem in the English language, at least any poem dealing with childhood and Christmas. It has been translated into almost every language, even embossed in Braille for the blind, and travelled to the four corners of the globe.

And as I delved into the subject, and unfolded the life of the author and his progenitors, I found that Santa Claus as we (and the world, for that matter) now know him is almost one hundred percent American. Not until St. Nicholas passed through the crucible of Doctor Clement Clarke Moore's mind and imagination did the patron saint of childhood ever ride in a sleigh, or have eight tiny reindeer with bells joyfully to convey him on the clouds and over the roof-tops of the world on Christmas Eve; nor was he dressed in furs, nor did he smoke a pipe, nor did he ever before get into the homes of good little boys and girls by going down chimneys, nor did he ever have

"... a little round belly,
   That shook when he laughed, like a bowlfull
      of jelly."

In fact, his true portrait had never before been drawn. One commentator calls the picture "the greatest piece of genre word-painting in the English language."

Then, another interesting bit of information was established: The prototype of our modern Santa Claus was none other than a little, rotund, always jolly Dutchman who used to do odd jobs around Doctor Moore's home, situated in the then rural part of old New York,—now known as the historic section of Chelsea in the modern city. This side of the picture seems very fitting, inasmuch as Santa Claus came to our land with the Dutch settlers of old New Amsterdam. In Holland he was known as the patron saint of childhood and the bearer of gifts at Christmas time; and the change of name from the St. Nicolaas, of the Dutch, is readily seen. In one country St. Nick was expected to come in at a window; he had some magic way of getting through the glass. In another land, stockings were hung on the outside of a door to hold gifts; in still another country shoes were used; but in each instance he was an unseen donor of gifts for good little boys and girls, and sometimes even for grown-ups. There was not much said regarding his costume; only in one land was he supposed to wear scarlet.

The Santa Claus myth begins with a real St. Nicholas, a noted bishop in Asia Minor about A.D. 300. As a saint of the Church his festival was celebrated on December 6th. His fame started on account of his generosity toward the three daughters of a poor citizen. On three nights in succession he passed their house, and each night he threw in a bag of gold as a wedding dower, which served to protect them from a degraded life. He was soon adopted as the patron saint of Russia, where, besides protecting virgins, he had children, sea-faring men and others added to his beneficent realm. Through the centuries his fame spread westward and his generosity became associated only with children, the same as the wise men of the East who bore gifts to the Christ Child in the manger; and with this transition came also the change of date to the historic December 25th.

Intrigued by these findings I said: "Come, if our modern Santa Claus is so essentially a new-world character, what was the background of the man who created him." This is the story.

Thomas Clarke, born in England, August 11, 1692, one time major in the British army, having served his country with distinction in the French and Indian wars in the new world, sought peace and contentment on a pleasant rise of ground, overlooking the lordly Hudson, in the rural section just outside of old New York. Rather late in life, in the year 1745, Captain Clarke married the vivacious Mary Stillwell, of notable English parentage. They twitted him about being caught in the bonds of matrimony so late in his career. In reply he hit his chest and, as if giving a command to his army, said, "The Clarkes, sir, never reach their prime, sir, till they touch sixty." He lived to

CLEMENT CLARKE MOORE AS A BOY

CAPTAIN THOMAS CLARKE
Grandfather of Clement Clarke Moore

MARY STILLWELL CLARKE
Grandmother of Clement Clarke Moore

see his five children become of age, so apparently there was truth in his statement.

The land that Captain Clarke acquired was the district that is now bounded by Nineteenth to Twenty-fourth streets and from Eighth to Tenth avenues, which then skirted the Hudson River. Here he set up his estate which he called "Chelsea" after the famous hospital by that name in London.

Later this gave character and color to this whole section of the city. Here Charity Clarke was born, the eldest of the Captain's five children, and it was she who later became the mother of the author of one of the best-known and best-beloved poems in the English language.

In the trying days of the Revolution (1777) the master of Chelsea was taken ill, and while confined to his bed, his house caught fire. Neighbors carried him to shelter not far away, but he died from exposure at the ripe old age of eighty-five years. Nothing daunted, the brave and determined widow Clarke set about building a new home for her children, placed four square to the winds that blow. Down one of the ample chimneys was to come a personage who was forevermore to be endeared to the hearts of old and young alike.

No sooner was the house completed than a number of American soldiers were billeted on the property. These men caused the owner so much distress that one of the officers reported the Widow Clarke's complaints to General Washington, who rode out on his famous white charger and gave the necessary orders for relief. While the American troops were there, a British vessel sailed up the Hudson, fired on the house and landed a ball in one of the partitions, where the mark remained for years. Mrs. Clarke was away at the time of the bombardment. Upon returning home in her chaise, a Yankee soldier met her and said, "Mrs. Clarke, the British have fired a shot into your house." "Thank *you* for that," she replied, laconically.

When the British took possession of New York, a number of Hessians were quartered in or about the Clarke homestead. The commanding officer proved to be so gentlemanly that he became a favorite with the family.

It was approximately at this time that a young man, who had taken orders for the ministry, became interested in the beautiful Charity Clarke, and revolution or no, he found his way out to the Chelsea estate, three miles from his activities in Trinity Church. The serious-minded young man was Benjamin Moore, who later assisted in officiating at the inauguration ceremonies of General George Washington as President of the United States; who read the last rites to Alexander Hamilton after his fatal duel with Aaron Burr; and who became the rector of Trinity Church and Bishop of New York, President of Columbia College (originally King's College), and, most important to the world at large, the father of the author of *'Twas the Night Before Christmas*.

If you care to walk along the south wall of old Trinity Churchyard, bordering Rector street, in New York City, you will see a small brown stone, not far from the graves of Alexander Hamilton and Robert Fulton. On this stone, which lies flat to the blue skies above, you will read this:

BISHOP
BENJ. MOORE
& CHARITY
HIS WIFE

[13]

The only child of these two was Clement Clarke Moore, born July 15, 1779. His early education was superintended by his father, and so apt was the son that we find him graduating from Columbia College in 1798, at the age of nineteen. He lived in the Chelsea homestead, which was amply large enough to house Widow Clarke, the Moores, and, later, the family of his own. He devoted himself entirely to the study of oriental and classical literature. He became proficient in French, Italian, Latin, Greek and Hebrew; and to lighten his severer hours he wrote verses which appeared in the *Portfolio,* and similar publications of the time. He was also musical, and had a flare for architecture, played the violin with great feeling and also the organ. He even drew the first plans for a church he helped to establish, by giving the land on which the edifice was built, and in which he became its first organist.

Moore's first separate venture in print was in the form of a tract published anonymously in 1804, and entitled: "Observations upon Certain Passages in Mr. Jefferson's Notes on Virginia." The "Observations," overcolored with religious

BISHOP BENJAMIN MOORE

Father and Mother of
Clement Clarke Moore

CHARITY CLARKE MOORE

CLEMENT CLARKE MOORE
Painted at about the time the poem was written

fervor, were not important enough, however, to retard greatly the reputation of the author of "The Declaration of Independence."

His next venture was also to be veiled in anonymity. He had a good friend who ambitiously studied law in the office of Alexander Hamilton, and one who later was to be referred to as "the very lofty, learned and accomplished John Duer." Moore and Duer entitled their book, *A New Translation with Notes of the Third Satire of Juvenal, to which are added Miscellaneous Poems, Original and Translated.* Duer was responsible for the translation of Juvenal, while Moore contributed an extensive "Introductory Letter" and the miscellaneous poems. In the literary reviews, of the year 1806, we cannot find that two new poets were hailed with enthusiasm.

Moore at this time was preparing for the ministry, but he was not ordained. His studies in this field, however, led him to compile the first work of its kind published in this country and was to put him in the forefront of American scholarship. The title was, *A Compendious Lexicon of the Hebrew Language,* in two volumes, published in

MRS. CLEMENT CLARKE MOORE
Wife of the Author

1809. With an abiding sense of humility, that endeared him to his many friends and students, he modestly states in the Preface of the first volume, "The compiler of this work is as sensible, as any other person can be, of its faults and imperfections. Yet he hopes that his young countrymen will find it of service to them, as a sort of pioneer, in breaking down the impediments which present themselves at the entrance of the study of Hebrew."

With the publication of this work his circle of friendships widened perceptibly. He became Doctor Clement Clarke Moore, and eventually was appointed professor of Oriental and Greek literature in the General Theological Seminary, to which he later donated the land now known as Chelsea Square, a whole city block in the heart of New York, where the towers of the Seminary are pleasantly outlined against the western sky.

Doctor Moore's interests in the advancement of knowledge and the general welfare of society led him into unusual fields of endeavor. We find him translating Tessier on sheep-raising from the French; writing a "Sketch of Our Political Condition" during the War of 1812, in which he vehemently asserts, "Let us then have peace upon any terms short of dishonor. This war, though not the only ill we suffer, is the great crying enormity which ought at once to be arrested." He addressed a pamphlet to "The Proprietors of Real Estate in New York," and signed it "By a Landholder;" edited two volumes of "Sermons," by his distinguished father; wrote a notable Address which he delivered before the Alumni of Columbia College; prepared an impressive lecture, "The Course of Hebrew Instruction," which was delivered at the General Theological Seminary; finally published his *Poems* in 1844; and last of all, a life of *George Castriot, King of Albania.*

Here is certainly a diversity of subject matter; but, out of it all, only one thing remains, that is the immortal *'Twas the Night before Christmas,* which, strangely enough, the kindly and learned doctor did not see fit to acknowledge under his own signature until twenty-two years after the lines were first written.

In the year 1813 Clement Clarke Moore was married to the beautiful Catharine Elizabeth Taylor, daughter of William Taylor, Lord Chief Justice of Jamaica, West Indies. The wedding ceremony was solemnized in old St. John's Church, November 20th. The talented and lovely young woman was only nineteen years old at the time, and her friends wondered why she selected for her husband a bookworm, and a man considerably older than herself. She replied to her friends later in a poem entitled, "Clement C. Moore — My Reasons for Loving," published many years after her death, which occurred at the early age of thirty-six. Nine children came of this union, and although six of these had been born before *The Visit from St. Nicholas* was written, only four could have listened with wide-eyed wonderment and delight as their father, for the first time, read the magic lines on the Christmas Eve more than a century ago.

There are several stories concerning how this masterpiece of "genre word-painting" happened to be written, but of all the authorities I have consulted, and all the members of the Moore family with whom I have talked, I like to believe the following version as related by a granddaughter, Mrs. Mary Moore Sherman, in her "Recollections," a copy of which was so kindly lent to me by Mr. William Scoville Moore, the great-great grandson of Clement Clarke Moore, to whom I am also indebted for copies of the portraits which appear in connection with this story.

In the year 1822 while Doctor Clement Clarke Moore was being driven back from New York to his sequestered Chelsea estate—and at this point one can easily imagine with his own sleigh filled with toys for his own children—the music of the bells on old Dobbin gave him an idea in their jingle for verses that might be recited before the great fire-place in his home. But who was to be the donor of all these gifts and trinkets? And then, perhaps in the same spirit as that other master of childhood's realm, Lewis Carroll, who was to come later and assert, "Just the place for a Snark," our genial doctor thought of the jovial old Dutchman, who did jobs about his place, as the model for St. Nicholas, and said: "Just the man for the piece."

So, on that memorable Christmas Eve, the poem was read before the fire-place—the same fire-place in front of which George Washington had undoubtedly stood many years before, and many other notables; because, according to the author's granddaughter, this "genial gentleman, scholar, poet and musician" held forth in "this spacious, comfortable house that was almost hidden from outsiders, surrounded by a large family," where he dwelt for many years, extending hospitality to many of the distinguished strangers who visited New York; and according to Philip Hone, one time Mayor of New York, extending the same hospitality to many of his own city, to the literary, musical, legal and ecclesiastical notables of the hour.

In the autumn of the next year the Moores had a visitor, a Miss Harriet Butler, daughter of the Reverend David Butler, rector of St. Paul's Church, which Bishop Benjamin Moore had dedicated several years before in Troy, New York. Miss Butler saw the poem and asked if she might make a copy. This she took back to Troy, and in a spirit of unrestrained enthusiasm sent the transcript anonymously to Mr. Orville L. Holley, editor of the *Troy Sentinel,* during the holidays of that year. The discerning editor immediately pounced upon the contribution and wrote a blurb to run in connection with it and the two first appeared in the issue of his paper on December 23, 1823. His editorial comment was as follows:

"We know not to whom we are indebted for the following description of that unwearied patron of children — that *homely* and delightful personage of parental kindness — Santa Claus, — his costume and his equipage as he goes about visiting the firesides of this happy land, laden with Christmas bounties; but from whomsoever it may have come, we give thanks for it. There is, to our apprehension, a spirit of cordial goodness in it, a playfulness of fancy, and a benevolent alacrity to enter into the feelings and promote the simple pleasures of children, which are altogether charming. We hope our little patrons, both lads and lassies, will accept it as a proof of our unfeigned goodwill towards them — as a token of our warmest wish that they may have many a merry Christmas; that they may long retain their beautiful relics for those homebred joys, which derive their flavor from filial piety and fraternal love, and which they may be assured are the least alloyed that time can furnish them, and that they may never part with the simplicity of character, which is their fairest ornament, and the sake of which they have been pronounced, by Authority which none can gainsay, the types of such as shall inherit the kingdom of heaven."

A copy of the newspaper was sent to Professor Moore (undoubtedly by Miss Butler), and it is said that the publication of the verses caused him chagrin and regret. They had been composed as a prank for his own children, and here they were published without his consent. Naturally, they were copied by many appreciative readers, reprinted anonymously by other papers of the country, and imitated by innumerable versifiers.* While they were written for only the children of the author's own fireside, they were to give joy to children of all firesides the world over.

With the re-publication of the poem at each Christmas-tide the desire of the public became more intense to know the name of the writer. It was not until the year 1829 that the editor of the *Troy Sentinel* announced that the author of the

---

* It is a tribute to Moore's poem that various persons have laid claim to its authorship, but no such claim was made until many years after the author's death.

famous lines belonged "by birth and residence to the City of New York, and that he is a gentleman of more merit as a scholar and writer than many of more noisy pretentions."

In those days it was the practice of many newspapers to print a "Carrier's Address" to be used in soliciting new and retaining old subscribers; and in this connection the poem was first illustrated by Myron King, a wood engraver of Troy, New York, about 1830. The picture shows Santa Claus with sleigh and reindeer riding over the housetops.

In the year 1837 an ambitious publisher issued the first book of its kind, entitled, *The New York Book of Poetry,* in which was included *A Visit from St. Nicholas,* but not under Doctor Moore's name, although it was of course known to his friends that he was the author. Philip Hone refers to it in his now famous diary, where he speaks of his "friend, Clement C. Moore, the author of 'The Night Before Christmas.'" And in the issue of the *Troy Budget* for December 25, 1838, its authorship was publicly acknowledged.

With the growing tide of popularity of the

verses, the learned doctor was led to include *A Visit from St. Nicholas* in his collected *Poems,* issued, as we have said, in 1844. In this book he has a line, phrased with his usual and becoming modesty, "My faint and timorous voice to raise." *Faint* and *timorous* indeed! It has echoed round the world.

And now we come to the first separate illustrated edition referred to in the opening of the story.

In the year 1848, there was a publisher—one Henry M. Onderdonk of 10 John street, New York—who apparently decided that the now well-known poem deserved a special presentation and dress. He consequently enlisted the services of an old wood engraver, T. C. Boyd, who had a little studio not far away on Ann street. Mr. Boyd was just another one of those serious workers whose name does not appear in the annals of American art; but in this case he has the distinction of being the first complete illustrator of the best-beloved Christmas poem in the English language.

If you look at the naïve illustrations, you will get an idea of the manner in which the old trundle-beds were used, after they were pulled from underneath the old four-posters, which were used by the head of the house and his spouse. And the picture showing Santa Claus in his sleigh, drawn by "eight tiny reindeer"—and everyone must admit that they are *tiny*—is more than likely a view of old New York, drawn from the artist's window, and showing the stepped-in roofs of the old Dutch settlers, and the pump in the middle of the road,—the latter being, undoubtedly, one of the reasons why the early citizens had to flee the city to get rid of the scourge of pestilent fever. Here is real Americana at first hand. And so, Mr. Boyd, in his quaint and simple manner, gives us glimpses of a dim and distant past, of days long gone by.

Doctor Clement Clarke Moore, after the death of his wife, lived for his children and for the benefit of society. The city moved out to his Chelsea estate, through which streets and avenues were cut. The hill on which his historic house stood was cut away in about 1852, to make new land and bulkheads along the Hudson River, and by the year 1854, according to one account, everything had disappeared completely, from its "flowery

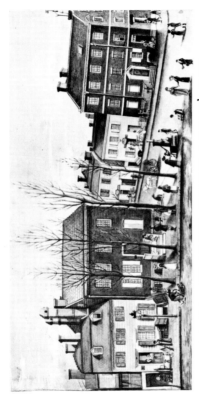

OLD NEW YORK DURING CLEMENT C. MOORE'S TIME

This is the corner of Greenwich and Dey streets. The spire of St. Paul's chapel is seen at the extreme right margin.

PAINTED BY BARONESS HYDE DE NEUVILLE

WALL STREET SHOWING TRINITY CHURCH BEFORE THE FIRE
One of the most authentic paintings of the period

grounds and grassy terraces." He built new homes for himself, and one of his married daughters, on the corner of Twenty-third street and Ninth avenue, hardly more than two hundred feet from his old homestead. He carried on his acts of philanthropy, deeding land to institutions, and donating sums of money — amounts ranging from five to fifteen thousand dollars — to worthy causes.

No better index to the mind of this kindly scholar can be presented than two paragraphs, taken from an address that he once delivered before the Alumni of Columbia College, as follows:

"The glitter and pomp of wealth naturally attract the multitude, while the worth of knowledge and wisdom lies hidden from the mass of mankind. But by making literature a badge of honorable distinction, it must inevitably become more attractive to the eyes of men. And as society advances in wealth and population, what better outlet for the busy, searching, restless faculties of man than the pure regions of intellectual cultivation, where the mind may become elevated above the gross, sensual, and selfish feelings of mere corporeal being. . .

"Whatever tends to draw men together in the bonds of harmony and friendship, is most desirable in this world of jealousy, suspicion, resentment, pride and coldness. . . . And if our association lead us to such feelings and to such thoughts, it will conduct us to what is of more worth than all the treasures of ancient and modern lore, to the love of our fellow-men, and to the knowledge of ourselves."

During the latter years of his life Doctor Moore bought a house in Newport, Rhode Island, where he spent his summers after he had resigned his professorship in the Theological Seminary. It was in his summer home that he died, July 10, 1863, just five days short of his eighty-fourth birthday. The minister who delivered his funeral eulogy said in the course of his remarks: "Modest, unpretending, retiring, always a learner, he seems to have striven to live only, as has been said of one who labored in another sphere, 'to love and be unknown.'" The good minister was hardly aware of the fame that was to follow.

The body was brought to New York during the period of the draft riots of the Civil War, when it was scarcely safe to convey anything in the streets. Covertly the casket was transported to St. Luke's churchyard, now gone, in Hudson street, where it reposed until the year 1890, when, on account of the sale of the property, Doctor Moore's final interment was made in Trinity Cemetery at Broadway and 155th street.

Several years ago a very happy and fitting ceremony was inaugurated. Early every Christmas Eve a procession of the devoted children of the parishioners of the beautiful Chapel of the Intercession, bordering the cemetery, march with banners to the grave of Clement Clarke Moore, and there carols are sung and a fresh wreath is laid on the final resting place of the modest author of the world's favorite Christmas poem for children.

Redrawn from the woodcut by Myron King

(1) OBSERVATIONS Upon certain passages in MR. JEF-
FERSON'S NOTES ON VIRGINIA which appear to
have a tendency to SUBVERT RELIGION and establish A FALSE PHILOSOPHY. New York, 1804.
Anonymous. (6 x 8½ inches.)

(2) A NEW TRANSLATION with notes of THE THIRD
SATIRE of JUVENAL to which are added Miscellaneous Poems Original and translated. New York,
1806. Published anonymously. (4½ x 7½ inches.)

*The "Introductory Letter" was by Moore, as well
as the contributions signed "L". The TRANSLA-
TION was by John Duer.*

(3) A COMPENDIOUS LEXICON of the HEBREW LAN-
GUAGE. Two volumes. New York, 1809. (4¼ x 7
inches.)

*The first work of its kind compiled and published
in this country; it put Moore in the fore-front of
American scholarship of his day.*

(4) A COMPLETE TREATISE ON MERINOS and other
SHEEP, compiled by MR. TESSIER. New York,
1811. (6 x 9 inches.)

*This was originally published in Paris. Two en-
gravings of sheep and two wood-cut plates were made*

for the book by Mrs. R. L. Livingston. The appendix states that Francis Durand claims "Proprietor and Translator." When Moore was elected to membership in the New York Historical Society on October 12, 1813, he presented his four "works" to the Society's library. On the title-page of this book he inscribes his own name as translator. It is interesting to note that more than a half-century later, descendants of the Livingston family made the claim that their great grandfather was the author of "A Visit from St. Nicholas."

(5) A SKETCH OF OUR POLITICAL CONDITION Addressed to THE CITIZENS OF THE UNITED STATES with out Distinction of Party. By a Citizen of New York. Printed for the author, New York, 1813. (48 pages, 5½ x 8½ inches.)

(6) A PLAIN STATEMENT addressed to THE PROPRIETORS OF REAL ESTATE in the City and County of New York. By a LANDHOLDER. New York, 1818. (64 pages, 6 x 9 inches.)

(7) SERMONS by BENJAMIN MOORE, D.D., Late Bishop of the Protestant Episcopal Church in the State of New York. Two volumes. New York, 1824.
    Edited by C. C. Moore as a memorial to his father.

(8) ADDRESS delivered before THE ALUMNI OF COLUMBIA COLLEGE on The 4th of May, 1825, in THE CHAPEL OF THE COLLEGE by Clement C.

Moore, A.M. New York, 1825. (44 pages, 5½ x 8½ inches.)

(9) **A LECTURE INTRODUCTORY TO THE COURSE OF HEBREW INSTRUCTION** Delivered in Christ Church, New York, November 14th, 1825, by Clement C. Moore, A.M., Professor of Oriental and Greek Literature. New York, 1825.

(10) **POEMS** by Clement C. Moore, LL.D. New York, 1844. (11 pages of front matter, 216 pages text. 5 x 7½ inches.)

> *This is the first time that Moore publicly acknowledged in print the authorship of "A Visit from St. Nicholas."*

(11) **GEORGE CASTRIOT** Surnamed Scanderbeg, King of Albania, By Clement C. Moore, LL.D. New York and Philadelphia, 1850. (5 x 7½ inches.)

(12) **A VISIT FROM ST. NICHOLAS**, By Clement C. Moore, LL.D., With Original Cuts, designed by Boyd. New York, Henry M. Onderdonk, 1848.

> *During the Christmas holidays of 1849, Onderdonk reprinted the wood-cuts in the December issue of "The Evergreen", a magazine of which he had become the proprietor. He also must have sold publication rights of the original book to Spalding & Shepard, because there is one known copy bearing their imprint in 1849, with different borders and a crude cover in color. The original 1848 issue is one of the rarest items in American literature.*

APPENDIX

A reproduction of a manuscript of *The Night Before Christmas* in Clement Moore's own hand (reduced). Courtesy of The New-York Historical Society, New York City.

'Twas the night before Christmas, when all through
      the house
Not a creature was stirring, not even a mouse;
The stockings were hung by the chimney with care,
In hopes that St. Nicholas soon would be there;
The children were nestled all snug in their beds,
While visions of sugar-plums danced in their heads;
And Mamma in her 'kerchief, and I in my cap,
Had just settled our brains for a long winter's nap;
When out on the lawn there arose such a clatter,
I sprang from the bed to see what what was the matter.
Away to the window I flew like a flash,
Tore open the shutters and threw up the sash.
The moon, on the breast of the new-fallen snow,
Gave the lustre of mid-day to objects below,
When, what to my wondering eyes should appear,
But a miniature sleigh, and eight tiny rein-deer,
With a little old driver, so lively and quick,
I knew in a moment it must be St. Nick.
More rapid than eagles his coursers they came,
And he whistled, and shouted, and called them by name;
"Now, Dasher! now, Dancer! now, Prancer and Vixen!
On, Comet! on, Cupid! on, Donder and Blitzen!
To the top of the porch! to the top of the wall!
Now dash away! dash away! dash away all!"

As dry leaves that before the wild hurricane fly,
When they meet with an obstacle, mount to the sky;
So up to the house-top the coursers they flew,
With the sleigh full of Toys, and St. Nicholas too.
And then, in a twinkling, I heard on the roof
The prancing and pawing of each little hoof —
As I drew in my head, and was turning around,
Down the chimney St. Nicholas came with a bound.
He was dressed all in fur, from his head to his foot,
And his clothes were all tarnished with ashes and soot;
A bundle of Toys he had flung on his back,
And he look'd like a pedlar just opening his pack.
His eyes — how they twinkled! his dimples how merry!
His cheeks were like roses, his nose like a cherry!
His droll little mouth was drawn up like a bow,
And the beard of his chin was as white as the snow;
The stump of a pipe he held tight in his teeth,
And the smoke it encircled his head like a wreath;
He had a broad face and a little round belly
That shook, when he laughed, like a bowl full of jelly.
He was chubby and plump, a right jolly old elf,
And I laughed, when I saw him, in spite of myself;
A wink of his eye and a twist of his head,
Soon gave me to know I had nothing to dread;

He spoke not a word, but went straight to his work,

And fill'd all the stockings; then turned with a jerk,

And laying his finger aside of his nose,

And giving a nod, up the chimney he rose;

He sprang to his sleigh, to his team gave a whistle,

And away they all flew like the down of a thistle.

But I heard him exclaim, ere he drove out of sight,

"Happy Christmas to all, and to all a good night."

Clement C. Moore,

1862, March 13th originally written

many years ago.